For Daniel and Benjamin Joseph

This is a Borzoi Book published by Alfred A. Knopf, Inc.

Copyright© 1984 by Nicola Bayley
All rights reserved under International and Pan-American Copyright
Conventions. Published in the United States by Alfred A. Knopf, Inc.,
New York. Distributed by Random House, Inc., New York.
Originally published in Great Britain by Walker Books, Ltd.
Manufactured in Italy
2 4 6 8 10 9 7 5 3 1

Library of Congress Cataloging in Publication Data
Bayley, Nicola. Elephant cat. (Copycats)
Summary: A cat imagines what it would be like to be an
elephant – that is, until bathtime comes. [1. Cats – Fiction.
2. Imagination – Fiction. 3. Elephants – Fiction] I. Title.
II. Series: Bayley, Nicola. Copycats.
PZ7.B3413El 1984 [E] 84-774
ISBN 0-394-86497-2

ELEPHANT CAT

Nicola Bayley

ALFRED A. KNOPF · NEW YORK

If I were an elephant
instead of a cat,

I would walk
through the forest
with a herd of friends,

I would use
my great strength
to push logs around,

I would carry
the prettiest seat
on my back,

I would have
enormous ears
for flapping,

I would have
an enormous trunk
for trumpeting,

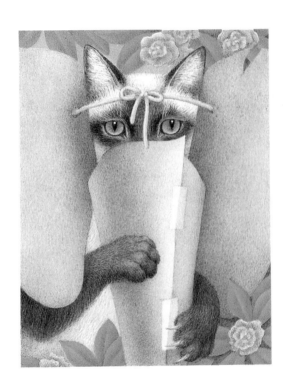

and if ever
elephant bathtime
came,

I would quickly
turn back into
a cat again.